The Don't-give-up Kid
And Learning Disabilities

By Jeanne Gehret, M.A.
Illustrated by Michael LaDuca

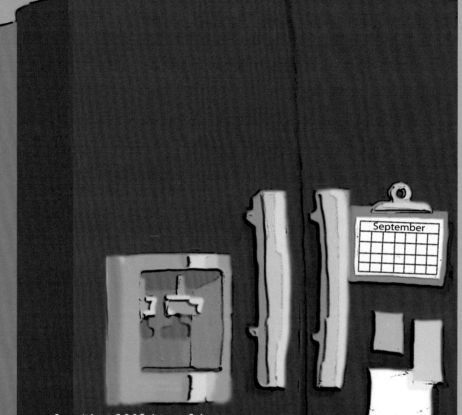

Special thanks to the Barton Breakfast Club,
where many ideas are born

ISBN 978-0-9821982-0-9

Printed with pride in the United States of America
First edition 1990
Fourth edition 2009

A BooksJustBooks book

VERBAL IMAGES PRESS ~ FAIRPORT, NEW YORK
Verbalimagespress@frontiernet.net
www.verbalimagespress.com
Orders: 1-800-888-4741

When Mom's making cookies, I can't think about anything else.

"Can I have a cookie, Mom?" I asked.

"Not now, Alex. I'm trying out my new grabber."

"Please? I'll clean my room...."

"You just don't give up, do you? All right, but only one."

Then she put the cookies up high where I couldn't reach them. I thought how her grabber would help me sneak a cookie, and went back later.

But I couldn't figure out how to use it.

"Can you show me how to use this, Dad?"

5

But I'll never be a good
inventor unless I can read.

7

Here's what happened on one of my worst days at school. "Hurry up, Slowpoke," whispered the girl behind me. It was my turn to read. When I stuck out my tongue at her, I lost my place. Then I found it, but the words looked like they were slipping down the page. Some looked backwards.

Nobody made a sound while I slowly read, "My hat is on pot of my head." The boy beside me started to laugh. Soon the whole class was making fun of me.

"On *top*, Alex," said Mrs. Sanchez. "Not on *pot*."

9

I don't like to read, even at home.
Dad said I just have to try harder.
"Come on, Alex, I've read
  Edison the Inventor to you
lots of times. Now you read a page to me."

10

A few days later, Mom took me to see Dr. Howell, who is a psychologist.

He asked me about school, and I told him how people laugh at me. "I guess I'm just stupid," I said.

Later, Mom said, "Alex, Dr. Howell says you're very smart, but you learn in a different way from other children. When most people read, the letters stay in one place on the page, but for you they sometimes jump around."

"You mean I'm the only one who has this problem?" I cried. "I'll never learn to read!"

13

"Yes, you will, Alex. When you want a cookie, you know how you keep trying one thing after another till you get one?"
 I nodded.

"Kids who learn differently need to try new ways to learn. I talked to the principal and they're going to let you work with Mrs. Baxter. She'll help you find your special way to learn."

And that's when things started to get better.

15

Mrs. Baxter helps three of us who work hard on things that are easy for most kids. Shelly is a good reader, but she needs help writing. Justin writes well, but he has trouble talking. Mrs. Baxter helps us all feel special.

Run

_un

She let me race the computer to practice reading. It showed me a word—*run*— and then asked me to rhyme it with a light in the daytime sky--*sun*! That was easy.

I scored several right answers before the words started to jump around on the screen.

It asked for the kind of bread you put your hamburger on. *Bun.* Or was it *gun?* Suddenly I couldn't remember what that word looked like.

Bun
or
Gun?

_un

Sun

19

Then Mrs. Baxter told me how one of Thomas Edison's inventions took more than 10,000 tries before it would work. Somebody asked the inventor, "How does it feel to have failed 10,000 times?"

20

"I didn't fail 10,000 times," Mr. Edison answered. "I found 10,000 ways that don't work." After many more tries, his invention was a big success.

If I want to be like Mr. Edison, I have to keep trying, too.

"Come on, Alex, don't give up," I said to myself, and concentrated hard on the word in front of me.

"B-un," I spelled carefully. Mrs. Baxter gave me a prize for beating the computer. I felt really good.

Mrs. Baxter won't let me give up on reading. Thanks to her, I've been reading Dad a new book about Thomas Edison.

Thomas
Alva
Edison

Did you know that Mr. Edison had trouble writing? Maybe he had a learning disability like I do.

Even a Don't-give-up Kid wants to quit when the going gets tough.

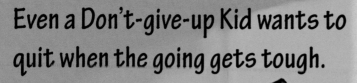

But if something's important to you, I guess you just have to keep working at it till you get it right.

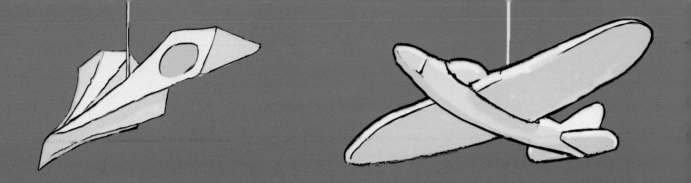

I'm going to finish that new Edison book all by myself.
But first I have to read about
how to see around corners.

And then my invention
will be complete.

For background on the author and inspiration for *The Don't-give-up Kid*, other books by this author, and more, see www.verbalimagespress.com.

Postscript to the Fourth Edition

In 1990, shortly after we learned that our first-grader might never learn to read, I wrote this book to give us all hope. Today, as a doctoral candidate in physical therapy, our son says of those early years, "Your love and care made me realize I was worth caring about." Your belief in these kids makes all the difference. Keep the faith!

—Jeanne Gehret, 2009

Learning and Attention:

Armstrong, Thomas, Ph.D. 2000. *In Their Own Way: Discovering and Encouraging Your Child's Multiple Intelligences.* Tarcher. Helps parents recognize eight different ways in which children can develop their gifts.

Gehret, Jeanne. 2009. *Eagle Eyes*, fourth edition. Verbal Images Press. Picture book for ages 6-9 showing the characteristics of ADD using a nature theme.

Gehret, Jeanne. 1992. *I'm Somebody Too.* Verbal Images Press. Novel for ages 10 and up from the viewpoint of Eagle Eyes' sister. Sibling rivalry and codependence in children.

Gehret, Jeanne. 2009. *Houdini's Gift.* Verbal Images Press. Picture book for ages 6-9 depicting a child with memory problems using a reward chart. Same characters as in *Eagle Eyes*.

Silver, Larry, M.D. 2006. *The Misunderstood Child*, fourth edition. Random House. Comprehensive, parent-friendly guide with extensive index.

www.interdys.org — International Dyslexia Association — Has branches and conferences.
www.ldworldwide.org — Learning Disabilities Worldwide — Has conferences and many online resources.

Thomas Edison:

Stross, Randall. 2007. *Wizard of Menlo Park.* Random House. Children's biography.

Wyborny, Sheila. 2002. *Thomas Edison.* KidHaven Press. Children's biography.

www.efwefla.org/bios.asp — About Edison's estate and laboratory in Fort Myers, Florida.

www.jhalpin.com/metuchen/tae/ehlai4.htm —Very early biography published by people who knew Edison; background information at an adult reading level.

Young Inventors and Problem-Solvers:

Biddle, Steve. 2003. *Beginner's Origami.* Viking. Beginner book on paper folding for youngsters.

www.odysseyofthemind.com — Odyssey of the Mind: Competitions using problem-solving skills for kindergarten through college.

http://firstlegoleague.org — Junior First Lego League for ages 6-9: Youngsters solving real-world problems through teamwork, research, and robots.

Discussion Starters

1. It takes time to make inventions and to change your way of learning. Look at the calendars, classroom decorations, and cookie shapes to figure out how long it took Alex to make his invention work and to do better in school.

2. What does Alex need to do in order to understand how to use the grabber? (pp. 3-4)

3. Why did the girl call Alex a slowpoke? Was he trying to be slow? How do you think he felt when the words seemed to slip around on the page? (pp. 8-9)

4. What mistake did Alex make when he was reading? Why do you think that happened?

5. Have you ever made a mistake in class? How did you want other students to react when you did?

6. Does Alex enjoy having stories read to him? Why do you suppose Alex doesn't like to read to his dad? (pp. 10-11)

7. Besides the directions for the grabber and the Edison book, what other things do you think Alex might like to read?

8. Look at what Dr. Howell says about Alex. (pp. 12-13) Do you think Alex is stupid? Why does he think so?

9. Alex's mother says when most people read, the letters stay in one place, but for Alex they sometimes jump around. How does Alex feel when he hears this? (p.13)